Rūdolfs

A well-behaved, responsible boy. He is an only child and his parents are getting divorced. Likes to play online games. Because he's been abroad a lot with his parents, he's good at languages and has a lot of friends on social media.

MĀRIS

Māris has younger sisters whom he often has to keep an eye on, even though he doesn't really want to. His mother is often out, and his father drinks a lot. When he gets a bit of spare time, he likes to browse the shops and imagine what it would be like to be rich and special. Plays he doesn't

THE NOISY CLASSROOM

POEMS BY **IEVA FLAMINGO**

ILLUSTRATED BY **VIVIANNA MARIA STAŅISLAVSKA**

TRANSLATED BY **ŽANETE VĒVERE PASQUALINI, SARA SMITH** & **RICHARD O'BRIEN**

THE EMMA PRESS
CHILDREN'S BOOKS

THE EMMA PRESS

First published in Latvia as *Skaļā klase* by Pētergailis 2015
© *Skaļā klase* by Ieva Samauska
Illustrations © Vivianna Maria Staņislavska 2015

First published in Great Britain in 2017 by the Emma Press Ltd
English language translation © Žanete Vēvere Pasqualini, Sara Smith
and Richard O'Brien 2017

ISBN 978-1-910139-82-0

A CIP catalogue record of this book is available from the British Library

Printed and bound in Great Britain

The Emma Press Ltd
Registered in England and Wales, no. 08587072
Website: theemmapress.com
Email: queries@theemmapress.com
Jewellery Quarter, Birmingham, UK

Supported by Latvian Writers' Union (*Latvijas Rakstnieku Savienība*)
and Ministry of Culture of the Republic of Latvia

Kultūras ministrija

CONTENTS

On Sunday Morning   1

I'm Sitting In A WiFi Hotspot   3

Friends   4

Archaeological Excavations (Year: 3014)   6

School Wants   9

One Of Many   10

A Promise   12

The Annoying Dinosaur   16

Nature Studies   19

Language Lessons   20

'I Don't Have Any Homework Today'   21

To The Loudest Boy In The Class   22

The Wind   24

The Boa Constrictor   26

The Day   27

The Medal   29

To The Girl In The Wheelchair   30

To A Boy In The Supermarket   32

I Like To Look In Windows   35

37	Even The Headmaster Was Young Once
38	Field Hospital
39	In The Twilight
40	A Day In The Teacher's Life
42	That Dragon
44	ASKfm
49	An Historic Mistake
50	Nature Studies II
52	Language. An Exercise With Difficult Words II
53	Alchemists Come In Handy
55	Chalk
57	The Schoolbag's (Secret) Contents
59	What They Don't Teach You In School
60	11th November
64	An Observation
66	The Noisy Class
68	The Christmas Market
69	A Wish
70	A Letter To Father Christmas
72	The Old And The New
73	School Holidays
77	**BONUS BITS!**

ON SUNDAY MORNING

A lonely, scarily shimmering ghost
sits slouched over a computer, like a man
who has just ordered a pizza in a café.
Although it looks as though the ghost
has been sitting like that all night,
it looks as though he likes it there.
If he already knows each nook and cranny,
this ghost – so lonely and scarily shimmering –
can he already get into them all?

A haunting, hungry ghost from a computer game
is waiting patiently for me to wake.

I'M SITTING IN A WIFI HOTSPOT

I'm sitting in a WiFi hotspot,
but nobody can call
or email me –
I'm very hard to reach right now,
apparently.

I'm sitting in a WiFi hotspot,
but only the leaves that
tumble to the ground
talk to me, and the two grey pigeons
eating from my hand.

I have been here for hours –
drifting like a castaway
from school to home and back again.
I sit here and I long, I long
for somebody to think of me today.

FRIENDS

I have so many friends,
when I try to list them all –
ten, twenty? More like five hundred! –
a single page is too small.

I have so many friends,
we can play games together all day:
Space Pirates, Mafia,
Words with Friends, trading cards…
Hey, what else can we play?

Even when it's late at night,
I can log onto Skype –
talk, sing, meet all my classmates,
do whatever I like.

I have so many friends –
but I still sometimes miss
meeting one special friend to play Scrabble.

And sometimes, that someone feels further away
than Latvia – can you imagine?

ARCHAEOLOGICAL EXCAVATIONS (YEAR: 3014)

And when they find
a tiny, tiny box in a jacket pocket,
with a wire coming out,
they'll all be wondering: what was this for?

Did early man use it like a toy,
a doll or a cuddly bear?
Or a telescope, to see the light and dark sides
of the moon, to look up at the stars?

Did early man talk to it like he thought
it had a living creature's soul within it?
Maybe it sang him night-time lullabies,
or was an ambassador from other planets.

Did early man love it so much, when he spoke
he thought it could hear it all?
Why did he keep it so close to his heart?
Was it thought to be part of his soul?

Did early man adore it so much,
this box that could do anything,
that he needed nothing more,
not even another human being?

Is it true early man was really a snail,
and this talking box was his shell?
How often did they look up into the sky?
Did they see the sun shine? Could they tell?

SCHOOL WANTS

School wants me to be like a calculator –
to come, to go, to do things, now – not later.

School wants me to succeed at every test,
learn all the answers, or at least to guess.

School wants my mind to rival God's perfection,
and never let mistakes escape detection.

School wants and wants, sends class alerts all day.
School doesn't ask how I feel today.

ONE OF MANY

The class is a many-headed dragon
that you wouldn't want to take on in a fight.
I am one of the heads
that has learned how to speak, nod and smile.

God forbid that I started to cry,
looked worried or hurt, sad or meek.
The others would all laugh their heads off at me:
what a wimp, a weirdo, a freak!

That's why I'm one of the many heads
who knows how to nod, smile and speak;
who buries their dreams and tears deep inside.
My laughter hidden from the rest
like golden butterflies.

A PROMISE

From the outside, it is perfect:
an almost flawless slab
of concrete, as if I were really made
of concrete, or even wax.

The slab doesn't show for a second
(perhaps I should call it a mask)
that I feel, that I hurt, that I have been hurt –
if anyone cares to ask.

As soon as I put it on at the school gate,
it sticks to my skin – close, close.
The mask confirms: 'I'm fine; I'm just
like everybody else.'

And everybody believes it –
my classmates and teachers too –
so I start to believe in it myself.
I nearly, nearly do –

Except that my own heart. Suddenly. Starts.
To whimper. And weep. And moan.
It weeps like a tiny sobbing child
who doesn't know which way to go…

Till one day, he makes his escape. He starts term
at a new school: new classrooms, new labs.
And he swears to himself that he'll study and live
without that old concrete slab.

WRITE YOUR OWN OBSERVATIONS HERE!

THE ANNOYING DINOSAUR

So here comes Cough the Dinosaur,
and he wants to give me his scaly paw.
He asks for a doughnut, a hot chocolate,
all with a gleam in his eye, then he sits
like a man getting into a theatre box –
and shows me how well he can cough.

He coughed on Monday, Tuesday, Wednesday
(of course, I took those days off school).
He coughed on Thursday, Friday, too.
(A whole week off? That's pretty cool!)

But when he tried to demonstrate his skills
on Sunday as well, I broke down, I yelled:
'Do you dinosaurs have no shame? Go home and think
about what you've done: you're meant to be extinct!'

NATURE STUDIES

It's what I really thought,
and so I wrote
that moths are, first and foremost, butterflies,
not just insects which like to eat your clothes.
Beautiful butterflies,
flying on gleaming wings.

The teacher said
both things were partly true.
The teacher got annoyed
that I had questioned her
and marked me down in Nature Studies
for daring to take up the case for moths.

LANGUAGE LESSONS

'Context' means life, not school:
above all I'm just living my life,
above all I'm just being me.
'Context' means Mum and Dad,
my brother, sister, Nan,
two cats, my dog,
my room with an orange ceiling
and colourful fish swimming
on the turquoise walls.
'Context' means my wishes,
all my daydreams.
But you say – do your homework!
You tell me – think of school
almost as if it were your only chance in life!
But above all I'm just living my life,
above all I'm just being me.

'I DON'T HAVE ANY HOMEWORK TODAY'

Mum doesn't get it, doesn't see or hear,
and Dad doesn't really have the first idea,
when they both thunder in to rain on my parade:
'I don't have any homework today!'

Do I have to get it engraved in marble?
Do I have to really, really bawl,
so that everyone nagging will hear when I say:
'I really don't have any homework today!'

He's cross, but he isn't a monster, my teacher –
although he might shout, he's unlikely to eat you.
He does have a heart, and it beats in his chest.
If Mum and Dad heard, would they give it a rest?!

TO THE LOUDEST BOY IN THE CLASS

To the First Violin in the whole school,
To the First Trumpet in the whole class,
To the First Desk-turned-into-a-drum-stool,
To the Most Enormous Chatterer,
Mumbler, Grumbler, Natterer,
Orator, Cheerer, Blatherer,
Burper, Farter, and Weird-Noise-Dispenser –
if he will let me;
please,
please,
SHUT UP ALREADY!!!

And stop thinking that you know it all!
Please, please SHUT UP
and LISTEN, could you, just this once, to the whole
 orchestra
that is the rest of us!
And, although you're not going to like it,
you should know –
you're not the first violin, or the last either.
In fact, you're just a common THIEF.
Yes –
a thief of SILENCE, which was full, unbroken, neat.
We're bored of you and all your cheek.

THE WIND

The hurrying wind blows through the school,
from one classroom to the next.
A moment in school without hurry
visits rarely and seldom stays.

The hurrying wind chases students
and teachers – it isn't fussy.
(I've just seen the headteacher get blown away.)
If anyone, anywhere's late – it gets huffy.

The hurrying wind can't be tamed – if you try,
it goes wild and blows worse than before.
All you can do is misdirect it
and leave it to run its course.

But some days, you can sit down in the corridor,
look out through the window at white clouds,
smile at the headteacher sitting next to you,
and watch the snow fall slowly, slowly
    to the ground.

THE BOA CONSTRICTOR

Slodze-Odze* is a huge fat snake:
it strangles children on their school lunch-break.
It coils itself round them and doesn't let go:
it wants to suck out all they know or can do.

Slodze-Odze makes them get out of bed
before the sun has even shown his head;
it makes each day a competitive race
and speeds them through like they're wearing skates.

Slodze-Odze strangles and continues to crush
until not a drop of blood remains.
At daybreak, the children were rosy and pink;
they were pale when the evening came.

It can't go on like this, Slodze-Odze,
you huge, fat lump of a snake!
I'm writing a letter to the DfE** –
the children are going on strike!

* 'Slodze-Odze' is a name Ieva Flamingo made
up for this strange snake. It literally means 'the
workload-viper' in Latvian, but that doesn't
quite work in English...

** The Department for Education

THE DAY

As long as my eyes can open,
as long as I'm breathing and hoping,
every day is a miracle,
every day is a surprise present –
the kind that's heaven-sent.
Every moment of it, like
the wind racing in all directions, seems to sing
I can do anything, anything
at all –
the Good, the Bad,
the Great, the Small –
whatever I wish,
whatever I choose,
and only me –
not teachers, or my parents,
or my Grandma Marge.
(Wouldn't it be crazy
to put her in charge!)

THE MEDAL

My teacher hasn't been to war,
but she wears a medal
on her left side; she keeps it near her heart.
Though you can't see it with the naked eye,
it glimmers like a star.

'For valour and bravery',
the medal reads.
It's one only a teacher can claim
who isn't afraid to stand up before a class,
or to slide down a chute at a waterpark –
it's for the truly brave.

Our teacher always has a smile,
a joke, a song. She challenges
the naughtiest kid in class to a duel
(over who can soar highest in a hot air balloon).
She goes to the opera after school.

My teacher hasn't been to war,
but she wears a medal,
glimmering like a star.
You can't see it with the naked eye –
it is our teacher's brave and loving heart.

TO THE GIRL IN THE WHEELCHAIR

She is almost, almost
exactly like me.

She likes to sing at the top of her voice,
scoop up armfuls of puppies,
read books, fly kites,
play hide-and-seek with the other kids.

She can count to a hundred in French,
bake a raspberry birthday cake for her mum,
blow the biggest bubble gum bubbles,
and wiggle her ears like a bunny.

I've seen her draw a dog and even a horse,
I've seen her tie a sailor's knot;
she knows where the Nile is, and once, at a fair,
she very nearly got lost.

She's almost, almost exactly like me,
though it's easier for her to play the spellbound princess;
but you mustn't imagine she's trapped by a dragon;
or think that her wheelchair's a frightening fortress...

TO A BOY IN THE SUPERMARKET

'Hello, you bright-eyed boy!
Why are you roaming the aisles
like you're moving through a gallery
full of pictures, some cheerful, some sad?
Where is your mum? Your sisters?
Have you come in for some milk?'

'My sisters are at home, my mum's at work,
and I'm watching the day go by,
just having a browse –
it's warm here, with all sorts of different people,
and I can think of all the things I'd buy
if I had lots of money.

I wouldn't want it all today –
there are loads of breakable things
that will just end up getting in the way.
But I'd definitely take that game,
that teddy bear, that motorbike,
and one or two other things my sisters might like.
And I would also have that gorgeous
pink swan-covered chocolate cake,
cumin bagels, an ounce of cheese,
some sausages and a raspberry lemonade.

I'd be really sensible with it –
and even if I just had the cake
for my eleventh birthday,
then my parents
wouldn't need to worry what to get me,
I'd be OK
with just one present.'

I LIKE TO LOOK IN WINDOWS

I like to walk and look in windows
when the evening twilight falls –
to see the lights go on and read
the stories I see inside.

I read them from the movements,
the silhouettes and shadows,
from the light bulbs and lamp shades
which help me give them titles.

I like watching the happy stories,
where everything's warm and bright –
roasting potatoes, steam rising off tea
and everyone home before night.

The sad windows also tell stories,
though they offer much bleaker views.
One day, they hope, things might look up;
but it won't happen any time soon.

Of course, I don't want to go on forever,
walking around the dark city.
I hope that one day, my own window will shine
with the light of a gentler story.

Then Mum would be home, and she'd have a new job,
and the kitchen would smell of pancakes,
and Dad wouldn't drink anymore (I'm sure of it);
he'd pass me a cup, and I'd take it.

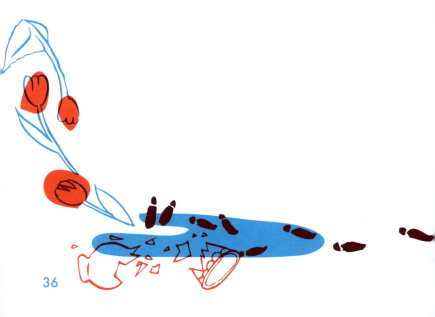

EVEN THE HEADMASTER WAS YOUNG ONCE

Even the headmaster was young once,
even the head went to school,
and the fact he'd become a headmaster –
he didn't know that at all.

Even the headmaster was scared of the dark,
and thunder and lightning;
got into trouble a thousand times,
for which he was given a hiding.

Even the headmaster skived off once,
and had bad reports up on his wall,
because – like I said –
that he'd end up headmaster,
he didn't know that at all.

If he had known, it's quite possible that
he'd have worried about his behaviour,
and it would have all seemed so improbable that
he'd have never become a headmaster.

FIELD HOSPITAL

When the bell rings and classes begin,
who is that shadow who holds a thick book
and creeps down the halls with a mysterious look?
He doesn't teach yoga, he's not a fakir
or a spy – he's just the school counsellor here.
He's always so sensitive, pleasant and kind –
he's every pupil's new best friend.
Anyone who feels no one's listening to them
can go to his office and whisper the problem.
Even the rowdiest boy in the form
once in a while trots along to his door,
then comes back feeling perked up,
encouraged – his cheeks glow brighter.
Because sometimes, every pupil's best friend
feels like their only port of call –
his office is like a field hospital
on a battlefield. Landmines, grenades blast outside –
but here with the counsellor, you'll be all right.

IN THE TWILIGHT

When the last bell rings at the end of the day
and footsteps, getting fainter, melt away
into the patterns of the outside world,
in empty corridors and empty classrooms
a couple of fairies play with their magic wands.
They lift them, wave them – spells fly through the air,
and nothing stays the way it was before!
Bing! Bing! – Scuff marks and mud go up in smoke.
Bing! Bing! – Disordered desks slide into rows.
Bing! Bing! – Stuck under desks, chewing gum
    mines get neutralized.
Bing! – And graffiti, 'Marta 4 Dean'.
When all the rooms are shiny and clean,
the fairies head home in the twilight.
But first, they hide away their precious tools
in the cleaners' cupboard, so no living soul
will ever know what they do in the school.

A DAY IN THE TEACHER'S LIFE

She could get on a train and get off in Portugal
or Spain – Santiago de Compostela
(although people usually walk there).
Or she could change her mind halfway and alight
at the Bay of Biscay,
rent a small house surrounded by green palms,
sip *aqua de Valencia*, go bowling,
play catch with jellyfish, sea urchins and crabs.
Make a canoe out of bark, go spearfishing,
pick mussels in icy waters, feel around in the depths
for a bottle like a slimy mollusc shell;

dig out a map, and go seeking hidden treasure;
escape a pirate ship, only just get away,
breaking free at the very last moment, diving into
a lagoon as blue as copper sulphate.
She could easily do all that, and most likely
she will one day –
but right now she is sitting at her desk,
tea steaming like an Icelandic geyser,
marking Class B6's essays,
every now and then glancing up at the curve of the globe.

THAT DRAGON

That dragon doesn't live in the woods,
in a palace, or in a cave.
That dragon lives somewhere much closer to me,
and – I have to admit – I'm afraid.

I haven't ever seen him up close –
not his eyes or his scales or his teeth,
but that dragon lives somewhere nearby, and at times
he shows up in my dreams when I sleep.

Sometimes I spot him out on the street
or snuffling behind the fence,
or I catch a glimpse as he scuttles away
when I'm spooked by the hiss of his breath.

Sometimes I can even hear him at school,
in the stairwells or stalking the halls:
you can tell that it's him by his heartbeat.
The dragon doesn't love anyone; it's said that he hates us all.

Sometimes I read about him online,
or I hear something on the news channel:
there's always more, since there's always a war,
a battle between Good and Evil.

There's always more, since there's always a war,
but this one will be over someday,
because Good always triumphs, and Evil will lose
and the dragon will die in his cave.

ASKfm

Whether you're laughing or crying,
if you're a boy or a girl,
ask, ask – today, not tomorrow –
be sure to give it a whirl!

What colour are your eyes, your hair, your phone,
  your hamster?
What would you say is your aim in life? And
  what's your background picture?
How often do you go to school? 1) every day, 2)
  frequently, 3) very rarely?
Would you rather have: a) a skateboard, b) an
  iPad, or c) a pony?
What do you notice first about people? Who are
  you similar to?
If I walked right past and, all of a sudden, just
  hugged you, what would you do?
Are there times when you want to forget about life,
  and just chuck it all in completely?
Are there ever times you feel dead inside? What
  is it that makes you feel free?

What do you do when you're sick of them all and
you'd just love to bite someone's face?
How are you feeling? a) amazing, b) pretending
it's all fine, or c) not great?
Do you like tuna sushi? And when you were small,
did you ever go butterfly-hunting?
What's the best thing that happened this week?
Did you see the first fly of the spring?
What's driving you nuts right now? 1) boredom,
2) anonymous, 3) me, or 4) something else?
How would you like it if now, right now, I just
came round to your house?
Will you send me your latest selfie? What do you
have on your keyring?
Where are you now? What are you doing? Where
were you yesterday evening?
Have you got a BFF? If you haven't, could it be me?
Are you happy? And, in the future, what would
you like to be?

Hi, hi, hi, I'm a follower of yours. If it's not too
  much trouble, then follow me too!
What can you do when there's nothing to do?
  Click 'Like' 50 times and a free gift will be on its
  way to you.
How do you know when you're in love? Feed your
  questions into *my* box!
If you answer right, you'll get a little red heart.
  And I'll stop writing, if not.

AN HISTORIC MISTAKE

I was sitting in a sumptuous chair
at the front of the assembly hall,
with people all round me, and still streaming in,
more and more – I could not count them all.
Oboes and trumpets were playing
a loud fanfare over our heads,
and they fanned me with peacock feathers.
I was wearing a crown
and a sash round my chest.
Perhaps I ought to clarify
the scene for the ignorant –
today was my inauguration
as School President.
Just then, as I opened my mouth
to make my first public speech,
the alarm went off in my bedroom
and the ceremony had to cease.
So, temporarily, at least for today,
the school was spared,
since my edict – 'Immediate Ban On All Lessons' –
had not yet been declared.

NATURE STUDIES II

Snow is a form of precipitation –
like dew, rain and hail.
Snow is Winter's fluffy coat,
which she wears with pride round the world.
Snow is a smooth and glistening mirror,
over which skis slip and slide,
and millions of snowflakes are falling
and no two are ever alike.

Hey, it turns out – isn't this cool? –
that I'm just the same – as snow!
Even if each flake is so very small,
it turns out –

that I am wonderful,
I am unique,
just how I am, like a

snowflake!

LANGUAGE. AN EXERCISE WITH DIFFICULT WORDS II

Analysis. Algorithm. Angst.
Rendezvous. Igloo. Astrophysics.
Paracetamol. Cambrian. Nuclear family.
Telepathy. Aqua-aerobics. Pronation.
Gastronomy. Optometrist. Cockatiel.
Barre chord. Plagiarism. Reading a thesaurus.
Übermensch. Fandango. Ubuntu.
Totem. Trullibubs. Gyroscope.
Camouflage. Emphasis. Bastille Day.

An exercise –
select two words, or even better, just one:
the one that speaks most clearly to your heart, or
draws you in with the strongest feeling
(like joy, hope, pain, the expectation of a miracle),
and try to understand why.

Alchemists come in handy, when you're seeking eternal life.

Like how eggs, milk and flour come in handy to make flat pancakes. But.

God forgive me, I have no idea where I'm supposed to put all those decimal fractions, logarithms, denominators, vectors, multipliers, roots and square brackets.

Every time I'm sitting in algebra class, I find myself looking at what's in my exercise book as if it were Chinese characters or messages from some omnipotent Martian civilisation and I never stop marvelling at its strange appearance, its mysterious nature, or how it behaves like nothing I've ever seen before.

Binomial, trinomial, polynomial, constants – every so often a secret codename is transmitted into the air, arcane signals are broadcast in conspiratorial tones.

Rather strangely, I sometimes think I understand what those Martian broadcasters are saying. When all their wires have turned incandescent and sparks, produced by an increase in voltage, have shot up into the sky like cold, glimmering stars. And the Martians, they can't, can't, just *can't* understand how I can now see and hear them – as if I were one of them! It makes me feel good. Because that means I've won!

A revelation dawns on me: even though I have no idea where I'm supposed to put all those decimal fractions, logarithms, denominators, vectors, multipliers, roots and square brackets, the doctor never takes anyone's appendix out without good reason. It's of vital importance to our immune system. And all things considered, it's the same with algebra.

CHALK

Chalk is dying. It's going the way
of the mammoth – extinct.
Schools don't need it these days.
The blackboard weeps,
the board-rubber bawls:
Oh where is he gone who was dearest of all?
They've still seen it recently
(it was just *there*…)
but now it's becoming exotic and rare.
A new morning's rising,
a new day is born.
The interactive whiteboard heralds the dawn.

THE SCHOOLBAG'S (SECRET) CONTENTS

I could bring the cat in with me,
or the parrot – a hamster, at least –
hoping they'd fit in between the books,
that they could be quiet and discreet.
I could stroke the cat in secret,
scratch him under his chin,
and no one, no one would ever know
I had smuggled someone in.
At break I would give him a saucer of milk
and let him out to play,
and – like I said – no one would ever suspect
with whom I was spending my day.
Yes, I could bring in the cat with me,
give him a rub-down and a pat;
then even if nobody else spoke to me,
he'd always be there for a chat.

WHAT THEY DON'T TEACH YOU IN SCHOOL

My phone is sensitive to touch:
it feels every tap and it won't make a sound
unless it knows my hands are around.

And I am sensitive to friendly looks,
which aren't difficult to notice
when they flow like a gentle brook.

Though frosty coldness sometimes
wants to wear a warm disguise,
you see the glitter of ice and snow in its eyes.

Whatever flames might flicker in eyes,
I won't be deceived or fooled,
because you learn about warmth in real life –
they don't teach you that in school.

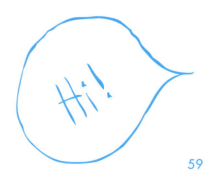

11th NOVEMBER*

I don't usually cry,
I don't like other people to see.
I didn't cry when I was stung by hornets
or when I trod on a nail,
but today –
today something happened.
When I was carrying my torch in the parade
with the rest, I looked over my shoulder and suddenly saw
that the light was shining so brightly
that it lit up so much more
than a single city street.

A tiny, glowing firefly at first – it became
a river which flowed and flowed, and which
could never, never be contained.
It flows, and over the darkness, the light surges;
an unexpected, secret bond emerges –

suddenly, I am a candle among
millions of similar candles,
embraced by the enormous light –
a tiny candle
in the hands of my country.

* Many countries hold special events on this day every year. In Britain, we remember the end of World War One. In Latvia, where Ieva Flamingo comes from, 11th November is also the date where people remember those who died in a battle for the country's independence.

AN OBSERVATION

The light eats up the darkness
until the last bit is gone,
and where the darkness used to be
a white brightness flickers on.
The light eats up the darkness
just like a strawberry;
a clear morning peers through the window
where the black night used to be.

The light is happiness, kind words,
calmness and friendship and love.
The dark is narkiness, anger,
and not caring, and bearing a grudge.
Look, look, at the light reaching out to greet it!
Look how it serves it up for you to eat it!

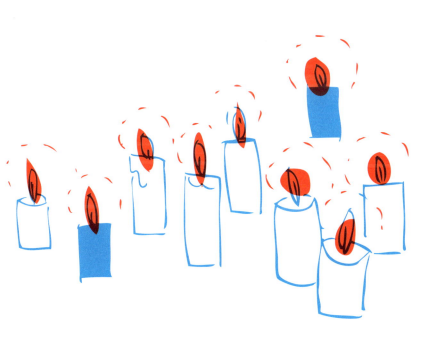

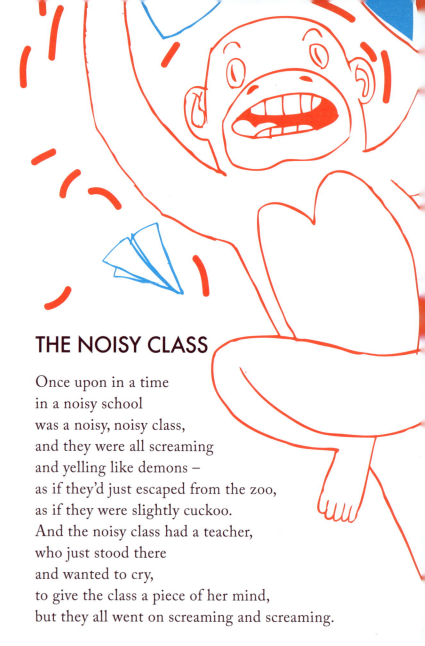

THE NOISY CLASS

Once upon in a time
in a noisy school
was a noisy, noisy class,
and they were all screaming
and yelling like demons –
as if they'd just escaped from the zoo,
as if they were slightly cuckoo.
And the noisy class had a teacher,
who just stood there
and wanted to cry,
to give the class a piece of her mind,
but they all went on screaming and screaming.

Then suddenly the door opened
and a little bird flew in,
as soft and pink as a sunrise –
and what did the bird do then?
Did he tell them all off? No – he sang.
He was quiet at the start,
like a warm, beating heart,
but then he got louder and louder
until suddenly, he caught fire
in a blaze of pink flames,
up by the light on the ceiling,
and he sang all the while as he burnt.

The teacher listened,
the noisy class listened,
and they suddenly started hearing
each other's heartbearts; from then on
they all started whispering.

THE CHRISTMAS MARKET

You could buy gingerbread there,
biscuit angels, bells, and lopsided houses
with words written on them in icing sugar:
'Jesus Is Saviour' and 'Love'.
The teacher was selling knitted gnomes,
sky blue socks and marzipan,
as well as red apples
and the thinnest crunchy wafers.
And I would have wanted so badly
to take home just some of it all
(even one gingerbread star),
if I'd only had a fiver in my wallet.
Do you want to know what happened?
That night, when I was walking home,
watching snowflakes fall in the twilight,
I put my cold hand in my pocket
and pulled out a little surprise –
a knitted gnome!

A WISH

If they would both just go for a walk
in the same place, at the same time

(Dad would stop the car and get out,
leaving the radio on really loud;
Mum would come out of her office,
head for the bus stop as usual,
then turn on her heel and walk in the other direction) –

if they would both stop thinking for a moment
about what the other one did or didn't do,
if they would both look up into the sky
and see a rainbow there
then each stand on their own side under it
and take each other by the hand –
Mum's hand so little, Dad's so big –
if only they didn't have to split up…

A LETTER TO FATHER CHRISTMAS

'Dear Father C,
or whatever your name is,
as far as predictions go,
this year I'm expecting a lot of
　　presents
(see my wish list, attached
　　below!)
and from you, this year, I don't
　　need much stuff,
just one big gift would be more
　　than enough:
I would really love it if, instead
　　of an iPod
(which I'm getting from Dad),
you could give me… a gnome!

But not the common or garden kind,
knitted or painted,
not some kind of PhotoShop trick
or one you've pulled out of a barrel.
That's it: a real, live gnome –
the kind that does homework,
you know?
Yes, that would be the very best present of all,
considering how busy I am all the time.

P.S.
I hope this won't be too difficult on your end.

Send!'

THE OLD AND THE NEW

The old –
tired,
its hands full of heavy bags and parcels,
its shoulders hunched,
stands in the doorway bidding everyone goodbye.

The new –
with a bright blue tit on its shoulder,
is fidgeting impatiently,
hopping from one foot to the other,
peering through a crack
at all of us inside.

When the old goes away,
when it disappears, the footprints it left start to vanish,
until not even the faintest shadow remains.
The new blows bubble gum from both of its ears,
stands on its head
and cheerfully calls out,
'Happy New Year! I wish you all the best!' –
does the splits, turns a triple somersault,
then finally lands, feet firmly on the ground,
and (with the blue tit still on its shoulder),
steps into the house.

SCHOOL HOLIDAYS

Away with cages, coops and traps, and other kinds
    of snares!
When it's the holidays, you're fully freed from all
    these cares!

Free from numbers, counting, theorems,
science projects, choir practice, diagrams and
    ecosystems,
from having to pick the right answer, getting up so
    early it's bad for your health,
from mediocrity, average marks, other countries'
    stories and myths,

from anticyclones, teachers' mood swings,
wailing, bleating, all the other background noise
    that does your head in,
from supposed crushes and/or funny tummies,
from fighting to be heard or – keeping schtum,
free, released and totally chilled,
like a twenty-stone weight has been lifted,
and as easy as ticking the right answer:
a) A bird
b) A butterfly
c) The flash of a comet –
you're shooting off, the blue sky in the distance!

During school holidays, time races, jumps,
    crawls, dashes,
chirrups and bubbles, skips, strides,
sparkles with joy like a glowing firefly.
Time on holiday
quivers,
sways and flutters and flies –
free as a bird, a grasshopper, a squirrel, a dolphin,
an earthworm,
it is ALIVE.

THE NOISY CLASSROOM

BONUS BITS

- LEARN SOME LATVIAN 79
- ABOUT THE POET 80
- ABOUT THE ILLUSTRATOR 80
- ABOUT THE TRANSLATORS 81
- WRITE YOUR OWN POEM! 82
- ABOUT THE EMMA PRESS 87
- OTHER EMMA PRESS BOOKS 88

LEARN SOME LATVIAN

Now that you've read some Latvian poems, how about learning the language? We've picked out some words that were in the original Latvian text, along with how to say them (in brackets). Put the emphasis on the CAPITALS and try to roll your *rrr*s a bit.

- **skola** (scAWW-ler) .... school

- **draugi** (d*rrr*OWW-gi) .... friends

- **'Man nekas nav jāmācās'** (man ne-KASS now YAH-maht-sahs) ... 'I don't have any homework today'

- **skolotājs** (scOL-ot-ice) .... male teacher

- **skolotāja** (scOL-ot-eye) .... female teacher

- **direktors** (DI*RRR*-ek-to*rrr*s) .... headteacher

- **zāle** (ZAAA-leh) .... assembly hall

- **tāfelīte** (TAH-fuh-lee-tuh) .... whiteboard

- **soma** (SORE-mah) .... schoolbag

- **brīvlaiks** (B*RRR*EEV-likes) .... holidays

- **zīmulis** (ZEE-mul-isss) .... pencil

ABOUT THE POET

Ieva Flamingo (the pen name of Ieva Samauska) is one of the most prolific Latvian children's authors writing today. She has been a journalist at various newspapers and magazines for over twenty years, and for the last ten years has worked at *Ieva*, Latvia's biggest weekly magazine. She won the Pastariņš Prize for Latvian Children's Literature in 2015 and her books have been nominated for the International Jānis Baltvilks Baltic Sea Region Award four times. Her first collection of lyrical poems, *Kā uzburt sniegu/How to conjure up snow* (liels un mazs, 2006), was adapted for the Latvian National Theatre in 2007. Ieva lives in Saldus, a small town in Latvia, with her family, three cats and a white dog.

ABOUT THE ILLUSTRATOR

Vivianna Maria Staņislavska studied Printmaking and Graphic Arts at the Art Academy of Latvia. *The Noisy Classroom* is her debut illustrated book and won her the Jānis Baltvilks 'Jaunaudze' Award in 2016.

ABOUT THE TRANSLATORS

Žanete Vēvere Pasqualini works as a literary agent for Latvian Literature and translates in her spare time. Her translation of Kristine Ulberga's *The Green Crow* is forthcoming from Peter Owen Publishers, and she translated several stories for *The Book of Riga*, forthcoming from Comma Press.

Sara Smith studied Italian and Business at Edinburgh University, where she was awarded a Swiss Arts Council prize. She lives in Rome and works as a teacher and translator, and her work has been published by *Guerra Editori*, *Artes Faveo* and *Compagnia Editoriale*.

Richard O'Brien is an editor at the Emma Press, and in 2017 won an Eric Gregory Award for his own poetry. Richard has published three pamphlets, and also writes poetry and plays for children. He especially enjoyed finding ways to preserve Ieva's rhymes and rhythms in this English version.

WRITE YOUR OWN POEM!

Fancy writing your own poem and then maybe illustrating it too? Translator Richard O'Brien has come up with some ideas to help get you started.

In 'Nature Studies' (p. 19), a pupil gets in trouble with the teacher for defending the moth. What animal, insect or plant do you feel has an unfair reputation? How could you put a positive spin on this creature? Write a poem defending the subject of your choice!

 Many of Ieva Flamingo's poems are about technology, and the difference gadgets and gizmos make to our lives. Have a think about an electronic device you or your family uses – for example, a TV, a tablet, or a mobile phone – and make a list of what's good and bad about it.

Then see if you can turn these ideas into a poem of your own – it could take one side, or be an argument between the two.

Adults are weird. We all know this. But Ieva has a good go at trying to explain how they might feel in poems like 'The Medal' (p. 29) and 'Even The Headmaster Was Young Once' (p. 37). Pick an adult, from your school (maybe don't use their real name!) or another part of your life, and write a poem which imagines what's going on inside their head. The fun of this is that you can't ever *really* know, so you can be as wild and wacky as you like.

In 'School Wants' (p. 9), Ieva creates the effect of non-stop demands by starting every verse with the same few words. Why not try this way of writing yourself? It doesn't have to be about school, but each section of your poem should begin with a repeated phrase. This could be anything, but here are some ideas to get you started: 'Mum says…', 'My brother always…', 'Breaktime makes me…'

Remember: in Ieva's poem, school – a thing which isn't a person – is described like it has its own wants and needs. This is called personification, and you could try the same idea.

Some of the poems – for example, 'One Of Many' (p. 10) and 'A Promise' (p. 12) – deal with difficult, sad feelings. Poems can be a helpful way to explore feeling different, or feeling bad, in a way that allows you to take charge. If you're not feeling OK, well – that's OK. But can you describe the feeling of lowness in a poem? Ieva writes about dragons and concrete masks. What images or ideas could you use to talk about sad or anxious feelings?

Not all poems have to rhyme, of course. But poems that use rhythm and rhyme are often very good at creating a sense of magic. In this book, 'The Boa Constrictor' (p. 26) and 'In The Twilight' (p. 39) play with rhyming words and patterns to do just that. There isn't *really* a snake in your school (and if there is, tell a teacher immediately...) but Ieva's rhythmic description makes you feel like there might be, in the larger-than-life world of the poem.

Choose a way of using rhyme (for example, either on every line, or every other line) and write a poem about something strange and amazing in your school.

In '11th November' (p. 60), Ieva writes about something unique to Latvia, which you might not have heard about before. Learning what matters to people in other places and countries can be really rewarding, so maybe you can return the favour and write about something special to you.

Is there something everyone in your country does on a certain day of the year, or something which people who come from a similar background to you all do? Or maybe just something you do with your own friends or family that you think Latvian children might be interested to hear about?

We'd love to see what you come up with in response to these prompts! If you'd like us to take a look, email your poems and pictures to hello@theemmapress.com with 'The Noisy Classroom' in the subject line.

ABOUT THE EMMA PRESS

small press, big dreams

The Emma Press is a Birmingham-based publishing house which makes books for adults and children. Emma Wright set it up in 2012 and works on all the books with her best friend from school, Rachel Piercey.

Emma Press books are starting to win prizes, including the Poetry Book Society Pamphlet Choice Award and the Saboteur Award for Best Collaborative Work. The Emma Press has been shortlisted for the Michael Marks Award for Poetry Pamphlet Publishers twice (2014 and 2015) and finally won in 2016.

The first Emma Press poetry book for children, *Falling Out of the Sky: Poems about Myths and Monsters,* was shortlisted for the 2016 CLiPPA (the Centre for Literacy in Primary Education's children's poetry book award), and *Moon Juice,* by Kate Wakeling, won the CLiPPA in 2017.

You can find out more about the Emma Press and buy books directly from their webshop here: **http://theemmapress.com**

ALSO FROM THE EMMA PRESS

Moon Juice

POEMS BY KATE WAKELING
With illustrations by Elīna Brasliņa

* WINNER OF THE 2017 CLiPPA *

Meet Skig, who's meant to be a warrior (but is really more of a worrier). Meet a giddy comet, skidding across the sky with her tail on fire. Put a marvellous new machine in your pocket and maybe you'll be able to fix all your life's problems. Kate Wakeling's poems are always musical, sometimes magical, and full of wonder at the weirdness of the world.

An Emma Press Children's Collection (aimed at 8+)
RRP £8.50 / ISBN 978-1-910139-49-3

ALSO FROM THE EMMA PRESS

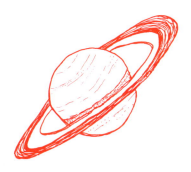

WATCHER OF THE SKIES:
POEMS ABOUT SPACE AND ALIENS
EDITED BY RACHEL PIERCEY AND EMMA WRIGHT
With illustrations by Emma Wright

How big is the universe? Are there dogs in space? What if your friend – or your granddad – was an alien?

Join the poets in wondering in *Watcher of the Skies*, a sparkling collection of poems about the outermost possibilities of space, life and our imaginations. Fully illustrated and accompanied with helpful facts about space, this is the perfect companion for any budding stargazer or astronaut.

An Emma Press Children's Anthology (aimed at 8+)
RRP £8.50 / ISBN 978-1-910139-43-1

ALISE

The tallest girl in class, Alise has a lot of style. She dresses like a tomboy but can still feel girly. Loves winter and everything about it, so her favourite poem is the one about the snowflake. Has a dog, and a parrot whom she's taught to speak.